FOR AUDIO,
THE GREATEST PERSON
I KNOW

Originally I wrote this book for my son, because I wanted to let him know that he should never stop dreaming. But after the book began to sell, it became somewhat of a phenomenon. I never anticipated the success I would have as a children's book author, the people I would meet, the places I would travel, and all the unbelievably inspiring stories I would hear. In the years since An Awesome Book! *was first published, I've been fortunate enough to achieve so many of my dreams thanks to the love and support of all the readers out there. My only hope is that in some small way this book can help inspire you to achieve yours . . . no matter how big!*

Love,
Dallas

An Awesome Book!
Copyright © 2008 by Dallas Clayton
All rights reserved. Manufactured in China.
No part of this book may be used or reproduced in any manner whatsoever without written permission except in the case of brief quotations embodied in critical articles and reviews.
For information address HarperCollins Children's Books, a division of HarperCollins Publishers, 10 East 53rd Street, New York, NY 10022.
www.harpercollinschildrens.com

Library of Congress Cataloging-in-Publication Data is available.
ISBN 978-0-06-211468-6

11 12 13 14 15   SCP   10 9 8 7 6 5 4 3 2 1 ❖ First HarperCollins edition, 2012
Originally published in 2009 by Awesome World LLC

AN AWESOME BOOK!

BY DALLAS CLAYTON

HARPER
An Imprint of HarperCollinsPublishers

THERE ARE PLACES IN THE WORLD
WHERE PEOPLE DO NOT DREAM...

OF ROCKET-POWERED UNICORNS™

AND
CANDY CANE
MACHINES

CANDY-O-MATIC 5000

AND MUSICAL
BABOONS

TRAINING PET RACCOONS

YES, THERE ARE PLACES IN THE WORLD
WHERE PEOPLE DREAM UP DREAMS

SO SIMPLY UN-FANTASTICAL
AND PRACTICAL
THEY SEEM...

OF DANCING WILD ANIMALS

WITH · DIAMOND - COATED WINGS

OF BUYING A NEW HAT

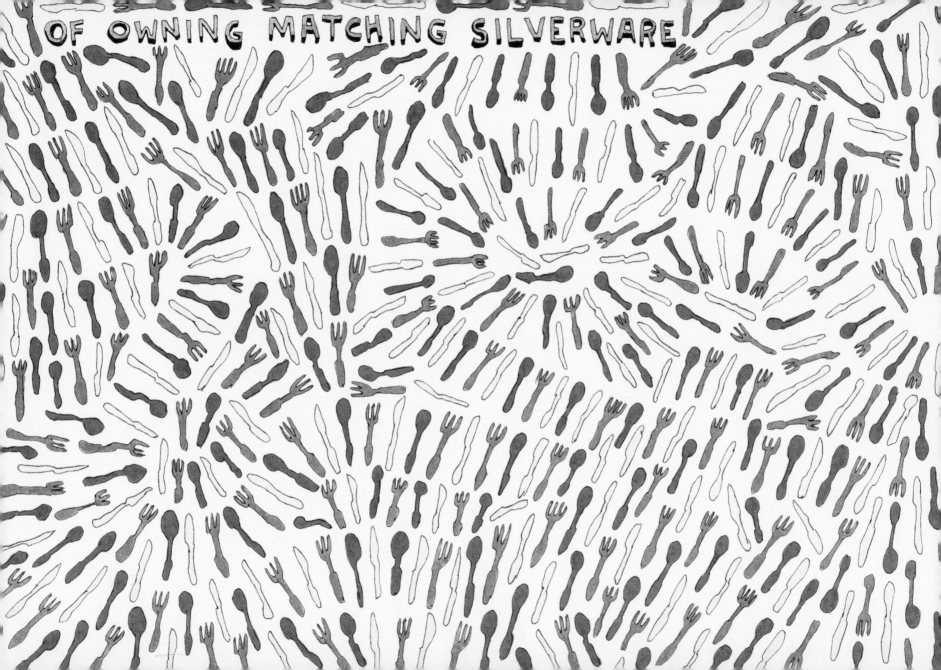

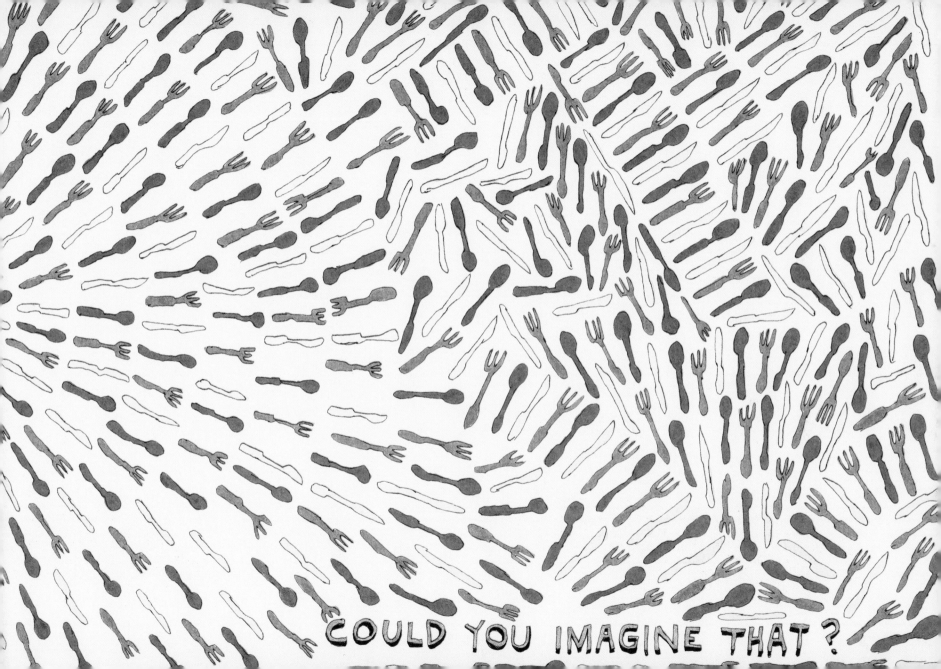

INSTEAD THEY LAY AWAKE AT NIGHT
WISHING FOR A CAR

THEY DREAM OF BREAKFAST SANDWICHES   THEY DREAM

OF TELEPHONES

SOMETIMES THEY EVEN DREAM OF DREAMS THAT AREN'T EVEN THEIR OWN

YES, THERE ARE PLACES IN THE WORLD
WHERE DREAMS ARE ALMOST DEAD

SO PLEASE, MY CHILD, DO
KEEP IN MIND
BEFORE YOU GO TO BED . . .

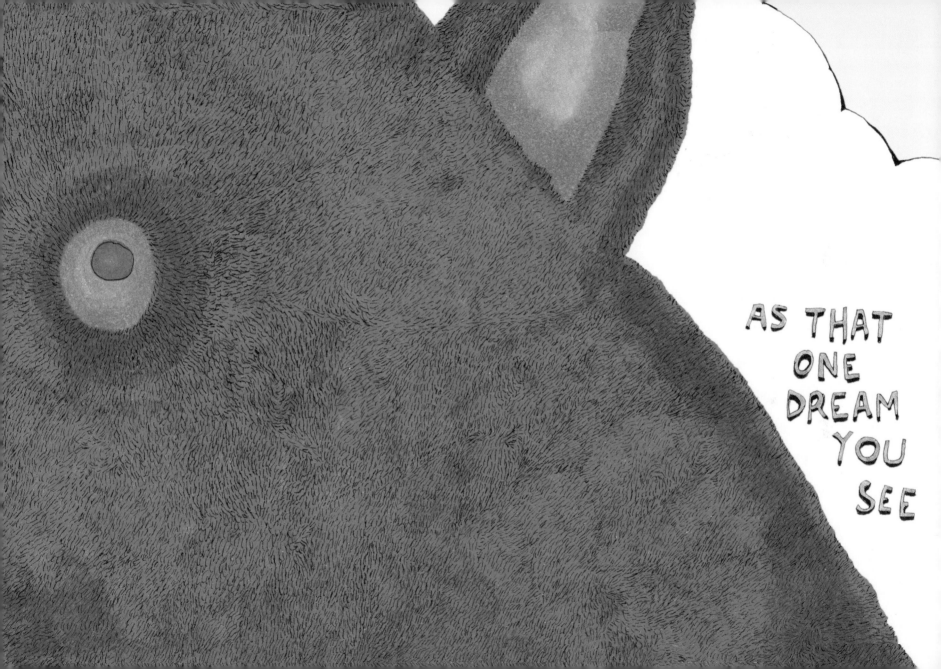

AS THAT
ONE
DREAM
YOU
SEE

THEN ONCE YOU'VE GOT THAT DREAM
IN MIND PLEASE DREAM A MILLION MORE

AND NOT A MILLION QUIET DREAMS, A MILLION DREAMS THAT ROAR

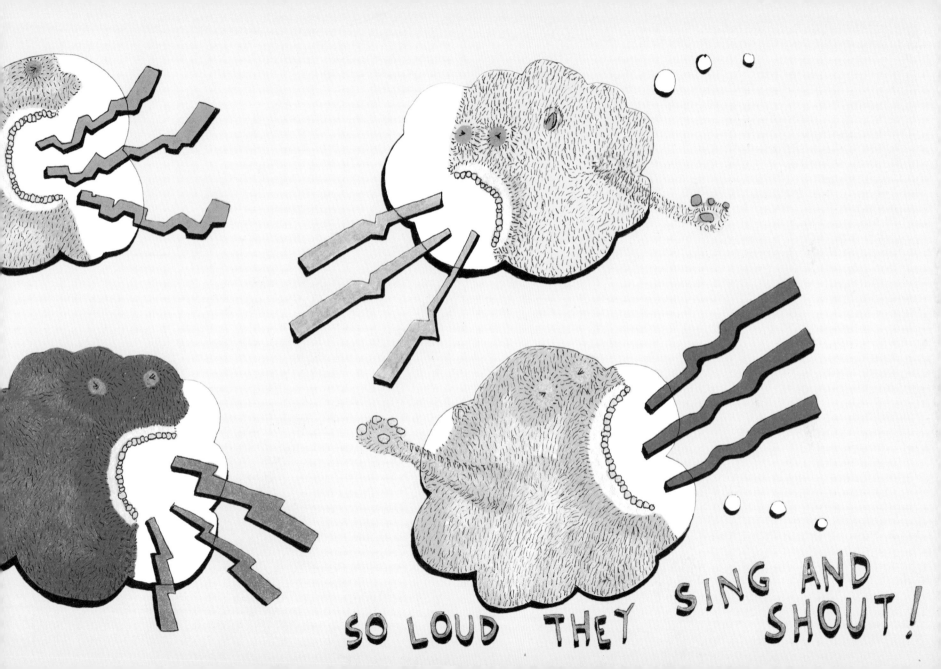

SO LOUD THEY SING AND SHOUT!

SO
SUPER HUGE
THEY SAY "HEY, WORLD!
GUESS WHAT I'M
DREAMIN'
'BOUT"

DREAMS SO BIG THAT THEY'VE GOT DREAMS AND THEY'VE GOT DREAMS UP UNDER!"

PLEASE DREAM FOR THOSE WHO'VE GIVEN UP

PLEASE USE YOUR DREAMS TO MAKE NEW DREAMS

FOR ALL THE DREAMS THAT DIED

AND THE WAY
THAT THINGS ARE NOT

AND IF THEY SAY THAT ALL YOUR
DREAMS SEEM TOO BIG TO COME TRUE

"THAT'S WHAT DREAMS ARE MEANT TO DO!

THEY'RE MEANT TO MAKE YOU SEEM
AS IF YOU DON'T KNOW UP FROM DOWN

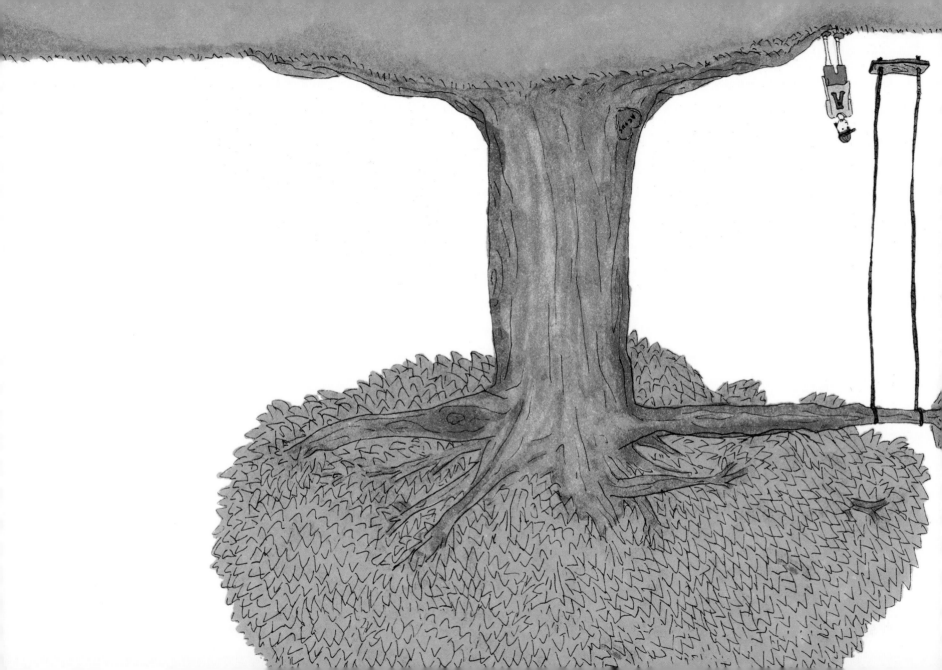

BECAUSE DREAMS ARE DREAMS
AND THAT'S WHY DREAMS ARE
WORTH HAVING AROUND!

JUST REMEMBER
WHAT I SAID

"CLOSE YOUR EYES, MY CHILD,
AND DREAM
THAT PERFECT DREAM
INSIDE YOUR HEAD"